Alice

Through The Wormhole

Alice Through The Wormhole

Alice

Through The Wormhole

by Tim Fisher

Illustrated by Conor Murphy

Published by Oxshott Press

Alice Through The Wormhole

Dedicated to

all children and parents

who are able to get the secret message

hidden in this book.

Down at the farm it was time for Alice and Luke to say goodbye to Aunty Margery and Uncle Tom. Alice and her aunty could hear her parents' car pulling up outside of the farmhouse.

The farmhouse was also run as a bed and breakfast and Alice loved helping her Aunty Margery out. Alice's aunt asked her to run down to the field where her Uncle Tom and younger brother Luke were cutting hay.

As Alice left the farmhouse and ran across the courtyard, Bob the sheepdog barked at her.

Alice looked at Bob and nodded her head. She knew that now her brother had come of age. It was time to let him in on the secret!

Alice made her way across the field and told Luke that their mom and dad had arrived to take them back home.

As Alice, Luke, and Uncle Tom headed towards the farmhouse Luke said, "Thanks for all the tractor rides! I've had a great weekend. When I get back to school I'll tell all my friends that when I grow up I want to be a farmer just like my Uncle Tom."

Then Alice said, "Thanks for all the Cornish pasties and cream teas that we've had. When I get back to school I'll tell all my friends I want to run a farm house bed and breakfast just like my Aunty Margery."

They all laughed. As they continued across the courtyard, Bob the sheep dog kept barking and running back and forth. It was as if he wanted to coax them in to the old barn.

They walked on to the farmhouse. Alice heard her mother Wendy say, "I hope the children have been behaving themselves."

Their Aunty Margery replied, "Alice has been a marvel. She helped out with all the breakfasts and helped me change the sheets in all the guest rooms. She has been an absolute angel."

When they arrived, Uncle Tom said, "Luke helped me gather in the hay and gave me a hand with the fencing. I couldn't have done it without him. He has been a godsend!"

Wendy noticed Bob still barking. "He knows you're about to leave. You should make a fuss of him before you go," she told the children.

As the children left the farm house, their father Peter called out after them, "Don't be too long. We'll be leaving within the hour."

The children went across the courtyard to make a fuss of Bob.

Suddenly Bob ran into the old barn barking as if to summon them in. Alice and Luke followed him. Bob ran to the back of the old barn and scampered around the hay bales and into a stable.

It was dark but they could see Bob scratching the door of an old, decrepit, small horse-drawn carriage.

Golden rays of sunlight shone through the broken roof tiles. Once their eyes had gotten used to the lighting, they noticed that the side of the carriage was covered in cob webs.

Bob was now frantically barking and scratching the door of the old carriage.

Alice turned the handle of the carriage door. As she opened it, the rusty hinges creaked loudly. Bob jumped into the carriage, still barking as he scratched the door on the opposite side.

Alice and Luke followed Bob into the old carriage. Luke was amazed at the workmanship inside it.

To keep Bob quiet, Alice opened the opposite door. This revealed a strange circular window of mist that mysteriously spun around and around.

Bob the sheep dog jumped into the mist and magically disappeared.

Luke looked at Alice in shock.

They heard a voice from the other side. "Come on through," it said.

Luke said, "Now, that's a good trick. Not only did you make Bob disappear, but you learned how to throw your voice. Show me the trick. Go on, show me. Show me!"

"I'm not throwing my voice and I didn't make Bob disappear", Alice replied.

The voice shouted, "For goodness sake, will you two just come on through?"

Alice turned to Luke and said, "Don't be afraid. All will be explained. Just follow me through the mist. I've done this many times before and there is nothing to be afraid of."

Alice stepped out of the carriage into the mist and disappeared.

Luke said, "That's a great trick. Can I play?"

Luke followed Alice out of the carriage and into the mist, only to find himself, Alice, and Bob...

... in a strange land!

Luke looked around. "Where are we?"

"Don't worry," Alice responded. "I've been here before."

Bob said, "I have been trying to get you two here all weekend!"

Luke asked, "How are you throwing your voice so it looks like Bob can talk?"

Alice replied, "I'm not."

Luke put his hand over Alice's mouth and said, "Okay, now try and throw your voice."

"Relax, Luke," Bob said. "I can talk."

Luke removed his hand from his sister's mouth. He was amazed and told Bob, "Say something else."

"I really can talk," Bob said.

"Do you believe me now?" Alice questioned.

Luke was astounded. "My god, that's incredible!" he exclaimed.

Bob said, "I have been trying to get you two here all weekend but you both ignored me. Do you know how frustrating that is?"

Alice replied, "Yes, but I had to wait until the time was right to introduce Luke to the secret wormhole."

Bob said, "I have brought you both here for a reason."

Luke interrupted. "Where is this place and how did we get here?"

Bob replied, "I'll leave all the explanations to Olly."

The children looked up to see...

...Olly the owl perched in the bough of an old oak tree.

Olly the wise old owl began to cough to clear his throat. In a deep but friendly voice, he said, "Hello, children. My name is Oliver and you have just traveled through a wormhole. That's transportation through time and space from one side of the universe to another."

Bob interrupted. "Okay, enough about that. Alice can explain all that to Luke later. Just tell them why they are here."

Luke asked, "Are we prisoners here?

Olly and Bob started laughing. Olly said, "Heavens, no! Just walk back through the mist behind you and you will be back in your uncle's barn exactly where you all entered. Now, the reason Bob got you here is that we need your help. But first of all you must swear an oath of allegiance never to tell any other human about this place."

Alice was already sworn in so she stepped back.

Luke held up his right hand and swore never to tell another human. Once the ceremony was over, Luke asked, "How can we help you and what's your problem?"

Bob and Olly both looked at each other and shouted,

"WEASELS! DAMN WEASELS!"

"We're all frightened of weasels," Olly said. "Sometimes they attack us. You see, weasels are very sneaky. They have built a dam stopping the fresh water from flowing onto our land."

25

A duck came by and said, "Now there is very little water in our in our duck pond."

A frog hopped by and said, "It is very crowded in our frog pond."

A newt crawled by and said, "The water levels are critically low!"

Then all the animals said, "Can you help us?"

Luke said, "I wish I could, but our parents are about to leave."

Olly, glaring at Bob replied, "Before I was interrupted, it's because you have traveled through time and space to arrive here. Time in your world has totally stood still and will only restart when you return. But time here never stops. So your mother and father will leave with you both, and for them no time would have passed. Now, please. Will you both help?"

Alice asked, "Why have they built the dam in the first place?"

"They do let some water trickle down," Olly replied. "It's just enough to keep us alive."

27

A rabbit jumped by and said, "Me and my family have to dig lots of holes and plant cocoa and lemon trees."

A squirrel scampered by and said, "Me and my family have to pick all the cocoa beans and lemons off the trees."

A hare hopped by and said, "Me and my family have to jump up and down on the cocoa beans and turn them into dust, as well as squeeze the lemons to make lemonade."

A badger walked by and said, "Me and my family have to work all hours slaving over a hot stove turning the cocoa dust into chocolate."

Olly said, "Then the weasels collect all the chocolate and lemonade and deliver them to the Weasel King. He gets the Rat Queen to put a spell on the chocolate and lemonade to make it highly addictive. Then they use the chocolate and lemonade to

keep control of anyone who regularly needs and craves it. In fact, we have all heard stories about some animals neglecting their own families because they have to do nasty things for the weasels and rats. It's all to justify their craving for chocolate and lemonade."

Alice said, "In my world I heard my father saying anyone who tries to control someone, by supplying them with something addictive just for profit, should be taught a lesson. Why haven't you taken down the dam yourselves?"

They looked at each other and put their heads down in shame. Olly said, "We tried that once, but as we started to unblock the weasel's dam, they were waiting for us. It was an ambush. They poked us with sticks and bit us with their sharp teeth. It made us cry so we ran away. But they followed us back and took all our lemonade that we made from our lemonade trees. Now we have to hand that over every day."

Alice said, "They will only do the same to us that they did to you."

"Oh. no," said Olly. They're all frightened of humans. As soon as they see you two, they will be so scared they'll do as you ask. Everyone here has heard what bad things humans have done."

Alice replied, "It wasn't like this the last time I was here. I used to play with all the talking rabbits, badgers and frogs. It was beautiful. I did not know there was anything bad here, with weasels and rats controlling other animals with chocolate and lemonade. We will soon put a stop to this!"

With victory in the air, Alice and Luke headed for the weasel's dam. Everyone else followed at a safe distance.

As they started to unblock the dam, the weasels jumped out only to be horrified at the site of humans. Alice shouted, "Is this your work?"

The weasels said, "Oh, no. It was not us. It must have been the stoats!"

The stoats said, "Oh, no. It must have been the pine martins!"

The pine martins said, "Oh, no. It must have been the weasels!"

Alice said, "Enough! From now on you will all help with the work and share the chocolate and lemonade equally! And if we hear that you weasels have put the dam back, we'll be back!"

The sneaky weasels bowed their heads, though they kept saying it wasn't them. Finally, the dam was taken down. A chocolate and lemonade party started, with everything equally shared with everyone.

But Pink Eye, a nasty, sneaky weasel slipped off to tell the Weasel King what had just happened.

Now the Weasel King was called Three Bellies because he was the greediest and sneakiest weasel of them all. Three Bellies looked down on the nervously shaking Pink Eye, bowing and scraping in his cowardly way.

Three Bellies quickly wrote a letter which he put into an envelope with two pieces of chocolate. He sealed it with wax and stamped it with the royal seal. He ordered Pink Eye to deliver it to Splodge, the Rat Queen.

Pink Eye nervously made his way to the rat caves where he was greeted by guards. They shouted, "Halt! Who goes there and what is your business?"

Once Pink Eye had explained everything, the guards escorted him down to the throne room. He was presented to Splodge the Rat Queen who had just had a full-body make-over which included a mud bath, blonde hair extensions, pink nail polish and a leg wax.

Not wanting to ruin her nails, she asked Pink Eye to read the letter. Pink Eye slowly read it. The letter explained that Three Bellies wanted Splodge to put a magic spell on the two pieces of chocolate that would make whoever ate the chocolate turn into thieves, compelled to hand over all their stolen chocolate and lemonade to Three Bellies.

40

Splodge weaved her magic spell over the two pieces of chocolate. She told Pink Eye, "Hurry back to the chocolate and lemonade party and slip the two pieces of cursed chocolate into the children's pockets. When they get back to their own world and eat the chocolate, they'll be under my magic spell. Then they will steal all the chocolate and lemonade from their world. When that's done, they'll bring it back through the wormhole. Me and Three Bellies will have more chocolate and lemonade than ever before!"

Pink Eye hurried back to the chocolate and lemonade party just as it was time for Alice and Luke to be on their way. As they said their goodbyes, Pink Eye slipped one piece into Alice's pocket and the other into Luke's.

Alice, Luke and Bob went back through the wormhole and returned to the barn where their adventure had started. The three of them ran up to the farmhouse.

Alice and Luke asked if they could come up again next weekend. Aunty Margery and Uncle Tom both agreed.

"You're welcome here anytime," said Aunty Margery.

Alice and Luke jumped into the back of their parents' car with their weekend suitcases on their laps and said goodbye. Alice and Luke found the pieces of chocolate in their pockets and ate them. Suddenly their eyes went wide and misty.

It had worked! They were now under the Rat Queen's spell!

Bob instantly knew something was wrong. He ran alongside the car barking as loud as he could, only to hear Uncle Tom say, "Bob will miss the children. Look at him bark."

Bob ran back to the barn only to find that Alice had closed the carriage doors. This meant the wormhole was sealed.

On the journey back home, Alice and Luke sat quietly with their eyes closing, but still misty. Wendy said, "The children look sleepy."

As they pulled into their driveway, Peter said, "We're all back home safe and sound now."

Alice and Luke left the car and dragged their weekend suitcases up the stairs. Wendy said, "It's a school day for you two tomorrow so I want both of you off to bed."

The next day at school Alice and Luke went to see their friend who ran the school shop. Alice asked, "Who supplies the school shop with chocolate and lemonade?"

Their friend replied, "All the chocolate bars, crisps, biscuits, and pop comes from a warehouse on the other side of the village. They supply all the schools in the area."

Alice said, "You mean the one beside the old mill?"

Their friend answered, "Yes, that's right."

They waited until late Friday night when their mother and father had gone to bed. Alice and Luke put on dark clothes and quietly tip-toed down the stairs with their empty weekend suitcases.

They decided to cut across the meadow along the river bank and past the old mill where they found themselves at the school's warehouse.

Splodge the Rat Queen watched them through her crystal ball. She heard Alice say, "What are we doing here?"

Luke replied, "I don't know."

Splodge feared that her spell was beginning to wear off.

Splodge waved her magic rat claws to strengthen her spell. The children went back under her spell, unable to break it.

Alice noticed a window was left half open. She put Luke onto her shoulders and lifted him up. Luke climbed through to the office and found a bunch of keys. He took them to the side door and after several attempts, he found the key to open the door.

Alice entered holding both weekend suitcases, then locked the door behind her.

They were amazed at the amount of sweets, crisps, cans of pop, chocolate and lemonade. It was like an Aladdin's cave of sweets.

Splodge whispered into her crystal ball, "Just chocolate and lemonade, my darlings. Just chocolate and lemonade."

The children looked at each other, powerless to resist the Rat Queen's spell. As they both started to fill their weekend suitcases with chocolate and lemonade, Alice said to Luke, "Why are we doing this?"

Luke replied, "I don't know. I just know that we have to."

With tears in her eyes, Alice said, "But it's wrong to steal!"

Luke agreed, but they could do nothing about it.

Then they heard footsteps outside. A security guard flashed his torch light into the warehouse. Alice and Luke ducked down in horror. The security guard shouted, "I can see you. Come out with your hands up!"

Splodge, who was watching every move and not wanting to be deprived of her prize, weaved another spell.

Out of nowhere, Luke shouted out, "There's a gang of us and when we get out, we're going to give you what for!"

The security guard ran out shouting, "I'm going to get the police!"

Alice and Luke quickly filled their suitcases with chocolate and lemonade, then left. As they got home, they put their suitcases under their beds so it looked as if they had just packed to be ready for the coming weekend.

Soon it was early Saturday morning and the children were on their way to the farm on the morning bus. As the bus pulled up to their stop, they found Bob patiently waiting for them.

Bob saw that they were under some kind of spell and quickly guided them through the orchard. This meant they could not be seen from the farmhouse and could enter the old barn without being spotted.

Alice, Luke and Bob quickly jumped into the carriage and through the wormhole, carrying their weekend suitcases with them.

As they arrived, they were greeted by Pink Eye and his gang who knew that the children were still under the Rat Queen's spell. They ordered the children to open their suitcases. As they did, Pink Eye and his gang of weasels seized all the chocolate and lemonade and made their way back to Three Bellies.

Once they left, Digger the mole popped his head up from out of the ground. He told Bob, "Thanks to my network of underground tunnels, I've overheard everything that Three Bellies and the Rat Queen have been plotting."

Bob said, "Good work, Digger. I'll tell Olly. He will know what to do."

Olly said, "No need. I overheard every word. Children, you need to wait here. I'll be right back."

The children did so without question. As they patiently waited, Olly flew up to the top of the mountain and peeled off two pieces of bark from the cold magic turkey tree. It was called a turkey tree because the leaves looked like turkeys.

He flew back to Alice and Luke and told them to eat the cold bark. As they did, it loosened the Rat Queen's spell.

Alice said, "Oh, my goodness! What have we done?"

Olly told the children, "Don't worry about that, it wasn't your fault. Now take your empty suitcases and go back through the wormhole. Then fill them full of acorns."

Bob asked, "Why?"

Olly replied, "Just do it. I have a plan."

Alice, Luke and Bob went back through the wormhole.

They tip-toed out of the barn and went into the woods. After a while they had filled their suitcases with acorns, and brought them back to the barn.

They jumped into the carriage and returned through the wormhole. Olly was there waiting for them. He said, "Good. Now empty the acorns out and leave them here."

The children did as they were told.

Olly said, "You two must quickly go over to the rat cave and break the Rat Queen's crystal ball. If you are successful, you will never be put under her spell again."

Alice replied, "But I don't know the way."

Olly told Alice, "Put digger into your dungaree pocket and he will show you how to get there."

As Alice, Luke, and Digger made their way to the rat cave, Digger said, "We should all keep our heads down because I have heard through my network of tunnels that Three Bellies knows you've had the cold bark from the turkey tree. He's asked Splodge to increase her spell."

Meanwhile, Olly sent Bob to go across to Hogs Hovel and tell all the pigs and hogs that Digger had heard that Splodge had put a spell on all the oak trees. This meant as soon as the acorns hit the ground, they would magically roll from the floor and in to her rat cave.

Sabre the Boar King said, "Splodge told us that there was an acorn shortage and she would give us acorns if we let her have all our mud for her mud bath."

Bob said, "Olly has a plan. Splodge and Three Bellies are waiting at the top of hill. If you intercept the weasels and take all the chocolate and lemonade back to the entrance of the wormhole, you will find all the acorns you want. He's also arranged to have Splodge's magic crystal ball smashed, which means she will never be able to put a spell on you or your acorns again."

There was an almighty cheer as all the pigs and hogs charged to intercept the weasels.

Olly, with a bird's eye view, saw the cowardly weasels running away as the pigs and hog seized the chocolate and lemonade. They then made their way to the entrance of the wormhole.

Meanwhile, Digger guided Alice and Luke into the throne room of the Rat Queen. As they got near the crystal ball, the spell got stronger. This meant that the bark from the cold turkey tree was fading fast. Then one of the Rat Queen's guards heard them coming and raised the alarm.

They were soon surrounded by Splodge's guards. One of them said, "Look! They are still under the Rat Queen's spell. We can do what we like with them!"

One said, "Let's poke them with our sticks!"

Another said, "Let's bite them with our sharp teeth!"

Another said, "Where is Digger the mole? We have a bone to pick with him for telling on us!"

Alice, Luke, and Digger hugged each other in fear as the rat guards closed in. Then suddenly from out of nowhere, Olly flew into the throne room and pushed the crystal ball off its stand.

As it smashed into pieces, Alice and Luke were freed from the Rat Queen's spell. The rat guards started shaking in their boots.

Alice and Luke said, "Okay, if it's a fight you want, you have got one!"

The cowardly rat guards ran off in fear. Alice, Luke, and Bob made their way back to the wormhole. They saw Sabre shout to his army, "Well done! Now that we've returned all the chocolate and lemonade, there's a feast of acorns here!"

They all cheered as the acorn feast began.

The children, having been released from the Rat Queen's spell, packed all the chocolate and lemonade back into their weekend suitcases. Alice said to Luke, "If we hurry we can catch the same bus back home. It turns around at the top end of the lane."

Alice, Luke, and Bob jumped back through the wormhole and out of the carriage door that closed behind them.

They tip-toed across the barn through the orchard and caught the same bus as it had only just turned around.

Before long they were back at the school warehouse and replaced all the stolen chocolate and lemonade.

Then they ran back home and filled their suitcases with their weekend clothes and caught the next bus back to the farm.

Alice said, "I hope Splodge and Three Bellies haven't punished poor old Digger for helping us."

Luke said, "I think we'll soon find out."

He knew that after helping Uncle Tom and Aunty Margery down at the farm, there would be a new adventure as once again he will go with Alice though the secret wormhole.

THE END

Alice Through The Wormhole

ABOUT THE AUTHOR

Born in the UK, Tim Fisher moved with his family to Canada as a child, then back to England. He now lives in Birmingham, England, a region that seems to breed good rock and roll bands.

Tim is no exception. He fronts and writes the songs for VAN ROCKMAN, a UK rock band that has risen up the Independent Rock Chart to the top ten. In addition to his songs, through his company Red Fox TV Ltd., Tim has written a variety of projects including a radio series called THE ADVENTURES OF PC PERKINS and a series suitable for TV called TROUBLED WATERS.

He reports that writing ALICE THROUGH THE WORMHOLE was particularly thrilling. Currently, he is working on animating the story using green screen technology with animator Ryan Lowry and narrator Gemma Lewis. You can preview it and check out some of his other projects at:

www.redfoxtv.co.uk

ABOUT THE ILLUSTRATOR

Self Portrait: *"I broke my mask."*

Conor Murphy grew up in South Ockendon, Essex in the UK and currently resides in Bishop's Stortford, Herefordshire. From a young age he was good at drawing, and earned his BTEC in Graphic Design with an A grade in Art and Design. Unsure about art career opportunities, he spent years in a finance department. However, inspiration struck and he began to build his own artistic identity and shaped a career as an illustrator. His style is inspired by graphic novel art, with bold colour blocks framed by black line drawing.

He now works digitally, enabling him to work from his home studio with anybody, anywhere in the world. You can see more of his work at: *www.uncleconconz.com*

He likes hard rock music, video games, beer, comics, combat sports, nostalgic films, and Indian food. He has a golden retriever named Baloo, and a cat named Ruben. Unlike Alice's dog Bob, neither one can talk -- yet.

MORE TITLES FROM OXSHOTT PRESS

A boy learns from his wise grandfather that to love nature is to care for it. With emphasis on respect and love, THE BIG BLUE can be enjoyed by children and shared with parents and grandparents to warm the hearts of every generation.

Full Colour Illustrations, 33 pages

ALSO FROM OXSHOTT PRESS

A COLOURING BOOK ABOUT KIRA, AN ALASKAN PEREGRINE FALCON tells the true story of a peregrine falcon that was rescued from a traffic accident by volunteers of a raptor rescue organization in Alaska. Through informative text and images that readers can colour, the story explains how this amazing raptor healed from her injuries and went on to help educate people about Alaska's majestic birds of prey.

27 Fun Pages to Colour and Learn

ALSO FROM OXSHOTT PRESS

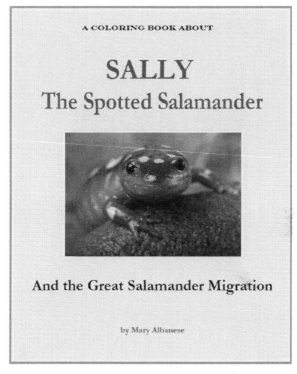

A COLORING BOOK ABOUT

SALLY
The Spotted Salamander

And the Great Salamander Migration

by Mary Albanese

This colouring book tells the true story about the amazing spotted salamander migration that takes place every year in the heart of the Sourland Mountains, a pristine preserve hidden deep within America's most densely populated state, New Jersey.

33 pages to colour and learn

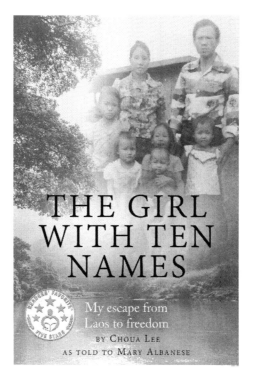

Meet Chua Lee, a plucky eight-year-old girl who in 1979 was forced to flee war-torn Laos. Escaping into the jungle with her family, she walked across her country dodging gunfire, landmines, and a deadly river crossing to make her way to freedom. Now she tells her incredible story. It is a story of courage and determination and a family's love that burned so bright that it guided them through a dangerous time.

A five-star READER'S FAVORITE.

52 pages

ALSO FROM OXSHOTT PRESS

"BERGBUCHLEIN, The Little Book On Ores" is an English translation of the first mining text printed, published between 1505 and 1518 in Germany. This historic text with its original woodcut illustrations and references to alchemy and astrology is a charming account of the early views on mining, metallurgy, and ore origination.

70 pages

Journey into the unknown with medium clairvoyant LORAINE REES. Coming from a long line of psychics and called upon by law enforcement to solve difficult cases, Loraine shares her gift to bring messages from beyond. Through the eternal bonds of love, she delivers a welcome answer to the age-old the question: is there life after death?

179 pages

ALSO FROM OXSHOTT PRESS

In this second book on the medium LORAINE REES, the clairvoyant works with a former Scotland Yard detective and a psychic sketch artist to explore astonishing truths from the other side, including the true identity of Jack The Ripper. She also helps to ease the troubled anger of a woman after death, revealing with stunning clarity how a soul can continue to grow and evolve even on the other side.

Loraine's detailed messages from the other side, verified by loved ones, are also supported by some shocking photographs. Her work gives great comfort to many as she reveals the bold truth of life after death.

201 pages

Printed in Great Britain
by Amazon